FROG ON HIS OWN

by Mercer Mayer

Dial Books for Young Readers
New York

For Father Yonov
and his family

Library of Congress Catalog Card Number: 73-6017
First Pied Piper Printing 1980
Printed in Hong Kong by South China Printing Co.
COBE
2 4 6 8 10 9 7 5 3
A Pied Piper Book is a registered trademark of Dial Books for Young Readers
A division of E. P. Dutton | A division of New American Library
® TM 1,163,686 and ® TM 1,054,312
FROG ON HIS OWN is published in a hardcover edition by
Dial Books for Young Readers, 2 Park Avenue, New York, New York 10016
ISBN 0-8037-2716-X

CITY
PARK

NO SWIMMING

HIC

CHIC

PUT TRASH HERE
PARK DEPT

EXIT